YUMA COUNTY
LIBRARY DISTRICT
2951 S. 21st Dr. Yuma, AZ 85364
(928)782-1871
www.yumalibrary.org

QUESTIONS EXPLORED

IS SOCIAL MEDIA HARMFUL?

by Tammy Gagne

BrightPoint Press

San Diego, CA

© 2023 BrightPoint Press
an imprint of ReferencePoint Press, Inc.
Printed in the United States

For more information, contact:
BrightPoint Press
PO Box 27779
San Diego, CA 92198
www.BrightPointPress.com

ALL RIGHTS RESERVED.

No part of this work covered by the copyright hereon may be reproduced or used in any form or by any means—graphic, electronic, or mechanical, including photocopying, recording, taping, web distribution, or information storage retrieval systems—without the written permission of the publisher.

LIBRARY OF CONGRESS CATALOGING-IN-PUBLICATION DATA

Names: Gagne, Tammy, author.
Title: Is social media harmful? / by Tammy Gagne.
Description: San Diego, CA: BrightPoint Press, [2023] | Series: Questions explored | Includes bibliographical references and index. | Audience: Grades 7-9
Identifiers: LCCN 2022029134 (print) | LCCN 2022029135 (eBook) | ISBN 9781678205027 (hardcover) | ISBN 9781678205034 (pdf)
Subjects: LCSH: Social media--Moral and ethical aspects--Juvenile literature. | Social media--Influence--Juvenile literature.
Classification: LCC HM742 .G33 2023 (print) | LCC HM742 (eBook) | DDC 302.23/1--dc23/eng/20220701
LC record available at https://lccn.loc.gov/2022029134
LC eBook record available at https://lccn.loc.gov/2022029135

CONTENTS

AT A GLANCE	4
INTRODUCTION	6
LEARNING MORE ABOUT SOCIAL MEDIA	
CHAPTER ONE	12
HOW DID SOCIAL MEDIA START?	
CHAPTER TWO	28
HOW DOES SOCIAL MEDIA AFFECT INDIVIDUALS?	
CHAPTER THREE	42
HOW DOES SOCIAL MEDIA AFFECT SOCIETY?	
CHAPTER FOUR	60
HOW IS SOCIAL MEDIA CHANGING FOR THE BETTER?	
Glossary	74
Source Notes	75
For Further Research	76
Index	78
Image Credits	79
About the Author	80

AT A GLANCE

- Myspace and Facebook were among the earliest social media sites in the early 2000s. Millions of users began sharing information about their lives on these platforms.

- Instagram became popular after launching in 2010. Some users even became famous as influencers on the app.

- Using social media can affect a person's self-image. Many young people depend heavily on the likes and comments they get from their online friends.

- Spending too much time on social media can lead people to compare themselves to others in unhealthy ways.

- Social media has become a delivery system for a lot of fake news. It is also a place where many people are bullied.

- Social media has added some good things to many users' lives. Many people who live far apart stay connected through social media apps.

- Some social media sites are trying to make users' experiences more positive. Some even offer users the option of turning off likes and comments.

- The people with the most control over social media are the users themselves. Setting time limits for social media use is one of the best ways users can make sure their experience is a healthy one.

INTRODUCTION

LEARNING MORE ABOUT SOCIAL MEDIA

Harper buckled her seatbelt. Just then, her phone dinged several times in a row. Before leaving the house, Harper had posted a picture to Instagram. It was the menu from the restaurant that she and her family were going to for dinner. She expected her friends to post drooling

Negative comments on social media can affect a person's self-image.

emojis. The restaurant had many flavors of cheesecake. But the alerts were not about the desserts.

Harper's brother George leaned over to see what was wrong. "Yikes," he said when

Many young social media users depend too heavily on comments and likes from online friends.

he saw the selfie of one of Harper's friends. "That haircut is not a good look on her."

"George!" their mother said from the driver's seat. "That's not very nice."

"That's nothing," Harper said. "You should see what people are commenting."

She felt more concerned as she kept reading. Her friend was going to feel hurt.

Then Harper's stepfather spoke up. He asked if she had ever gotten mean comments online. Of course, she had. Everyone was quick to share their opinions about social media. George said that he had gotten mean comments too. He said it was just how social media worked.

"But it shouldn't be that way," Harper said. "This can't be healthy." She remembered an assignment she received at school that afternoon. Her class had to write about habits that could hurt a person's

Posting something positive is a good way to combat the negativity found on social media.

mental health. Harper decided to write her paper about social media.

Her mother said this was a good idea. Young people spend so much time on social media apps. She worried that they cared too much about what other people thought. She also worried about safety. Many kids shared too much information online. She told Harper she looked forward to reading the paper. She hoped that Harper could learn something from it too.

"Maybe you could post something positive to your friend," her mother said. "Sometimes just one kind voice can turn things around. But then let's all put our phones away until after dinner." Harper had tons of great ideas for her paper. But for now, she was happy to turn off her alerts.

CHAPTER ONE

HOW DID SOCIAL MEDIA START?

The first social media sites were created in the late 1990s and early 2000s. People saw them as fun new ways to connect with others. Now friends could interact online. They could create profiles and share photos. They could send messages. Online users could even

Early social media sites offered users an exciting new way to connect with friends.

connect with friends of friends. They could make their online social circles bigger.

The most successful early social media site was Myspace. It came out in 2003. Myspace allowed users to be

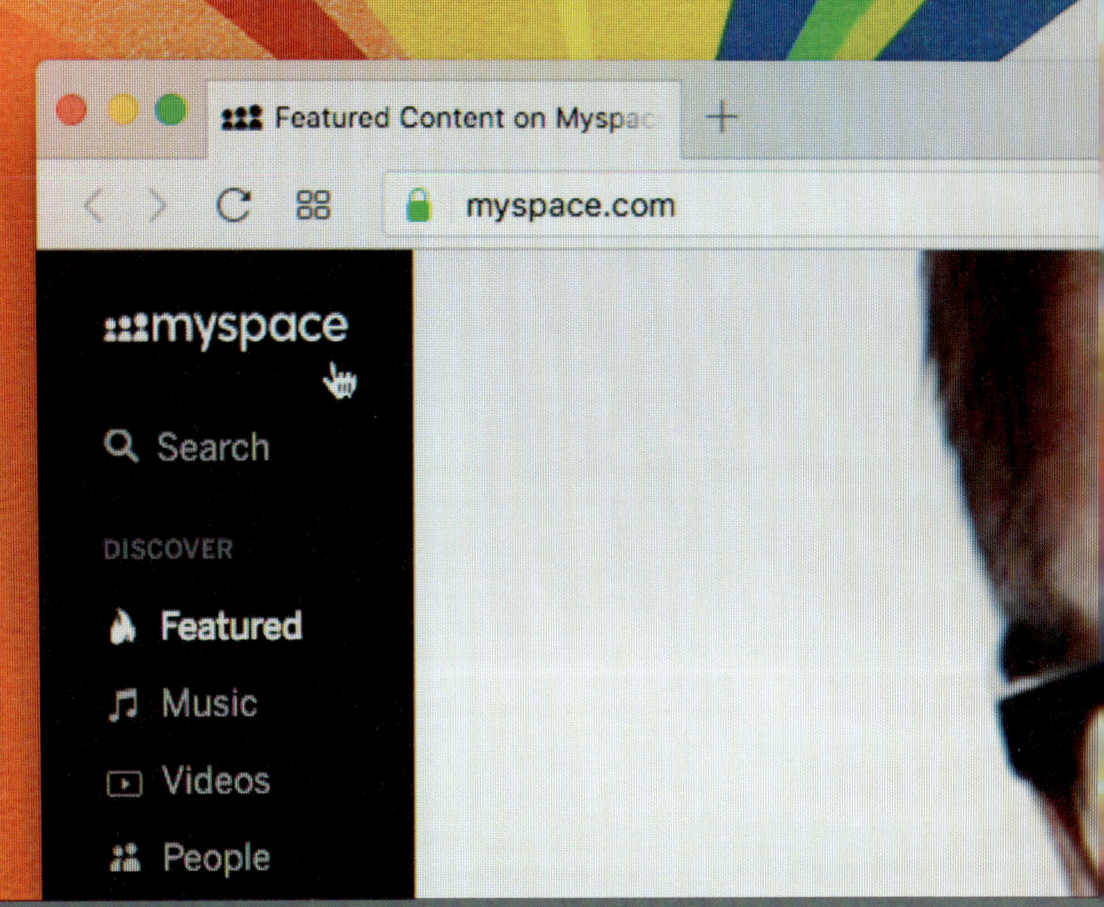

Some people worried about safety and privacy on Myspace. Fake accounts were just one concern.

creative online. Users could upload music and videos to their pages. Other people could leave comments on a user's page. Myspace became the most popular social network of its day. But some people worried about safety.

Many people made fake Myspace accounts with fake names. This meant users were not always who they seemed to be. Anyone who signed up for a Myspace page could see personal information that

DISGUISED IDENTITY

Megan Meier was thirteen. In 2006, she met a friendly boy named Josh on Myspace. But Josh soon started to bully Megan. She ended up taking her own life because of the cyberbullying. Later, people found out that a woman named Lori Drew was pretending to be Josh. Drew believed that Megan was spreading rumors about her daughter.

other users posted. Parents were worried about **online predators**. There were news stories about men who looked for young girls on the site. Predators often try to get girls to meet them in person.

FACEBOOK OPENS PARENTS UP TO SOCIAL MEDIA

Facebook came out in 2004. At first, it was available only among college communities. But in 2006, Facebook opened to anyone over the age of thirteen. Many parents were still worried about online safety. But Facebook had more privacy options. Users could make their accounts private.

Even though there was a minimum age for Facebook, many younger kids still joined the site.

This meant that only approved friends could see what was posted.

Facebook also set a minimum age of thirteen for its users. But this did not stop younger kids from joining the site.

Many parents post pictures or share stories about their kids on Facebook.

Many kids signed up for accounts without their parents knowing. Some even signed up with their parents' help. A 2011 study looked at parents who knew about their twelve-year-olds' Facebook accounts.

About 76 percent of them had helped their kids sign up.

Parents were using Facebook too. Many of them posted about their families on the platform. The site became an easy way for parents to keep family and friends up to date on their lives. In 2012, a survey looked at how parents used social media. More than half of parents shared news about their children's accomplishments on Facebook. As many as two-thirds shared photos of their kids.

Aisha Sultan and Jon Miller are journalists. In a 2012 article on CNN, they talked about parents on Facebook. They explained that these parents are telling their kids' stories without their kids having a say. Sultan and Miller wrote, "A permanent and public story has already been recorded about [the kids] before they have a chance to decide whether they want to participate."[1]

THE RISE OF THE INSTAGRAM INFLUENCERS

As smartphones became popular, social media became available in a new way. Users could visit Facebook through an app on their smartphones. Before, social media users logged on using computers.

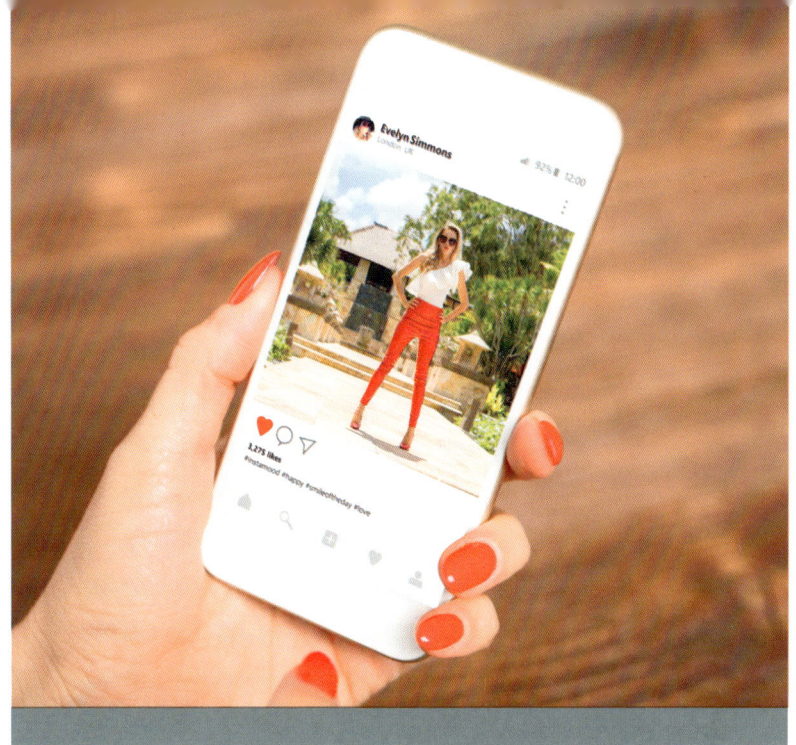

Instagram photos are often carefully chosen or edited. Many users post only images that paint a positive picture of their lives.

Now they could take social media with them everywhere they went. By 2012, about one-third of teens were using social media several times each day. Instagram was one platform they were using. This app came out in 2010. It focused on sharing photos.

Some people posted selfies with perfect makeup. Others wore designer clothing in their Instagram photos. These images were carefully chosen. They showed followers only what the user wanted them to see.

Users with the most Instagram followers became popular. They gained power because of this. If they wore a cool outfit in a photo, others wanted to buy one like it. If they used a new lipstick, others wanted to know where to find it. Businesses saw an advertising opportunity. Many offered to pay some Instagram users to post about their products. These users became known

Many social media influencers post about new trends or products.

as influencers. People followed them to discover new trends. Many young people wanted to become influencers themselves.

Jamie Bloch is a popular Instagram influencer. She knows that this job is not all fun. She spoke with *Psychology Today* about how overwhelming it can be. She said that influencers often feel limited about what they can post. Many do not feel like they can be themselves online. Bloch said, "If you don't know how to take a break or

DANGEROUS CHALLENGES

TikTok came out in 2018. It quickly became popular with young people. Users share short video clips. Many clips feature fun challenges such as lip syncing. But some challenges are dangerous. In 2021, the milk crate challenge encouraged users to stack milk crates. Users then climbed to the top of the stack. Many users who tried this challenge fell and got hurt. TikTok had to ban the challenge because it was so unsafe.

unplug from social media for a little while, there is no way you will be able to have continued success because no one can be 'on' forever."[2]

THE DISAPPEARING SNAPS

Snapchat came out in 2011. This social media platform had a new feature. Users could send Snaps to friends in the app. Snaps could be photos, videos, or messages. Once someone viewed a Snap, it went away. There were both advantages and dangers to this. It limited how much an image could be shared online. But it could also be unsafe. Kids were more willing to

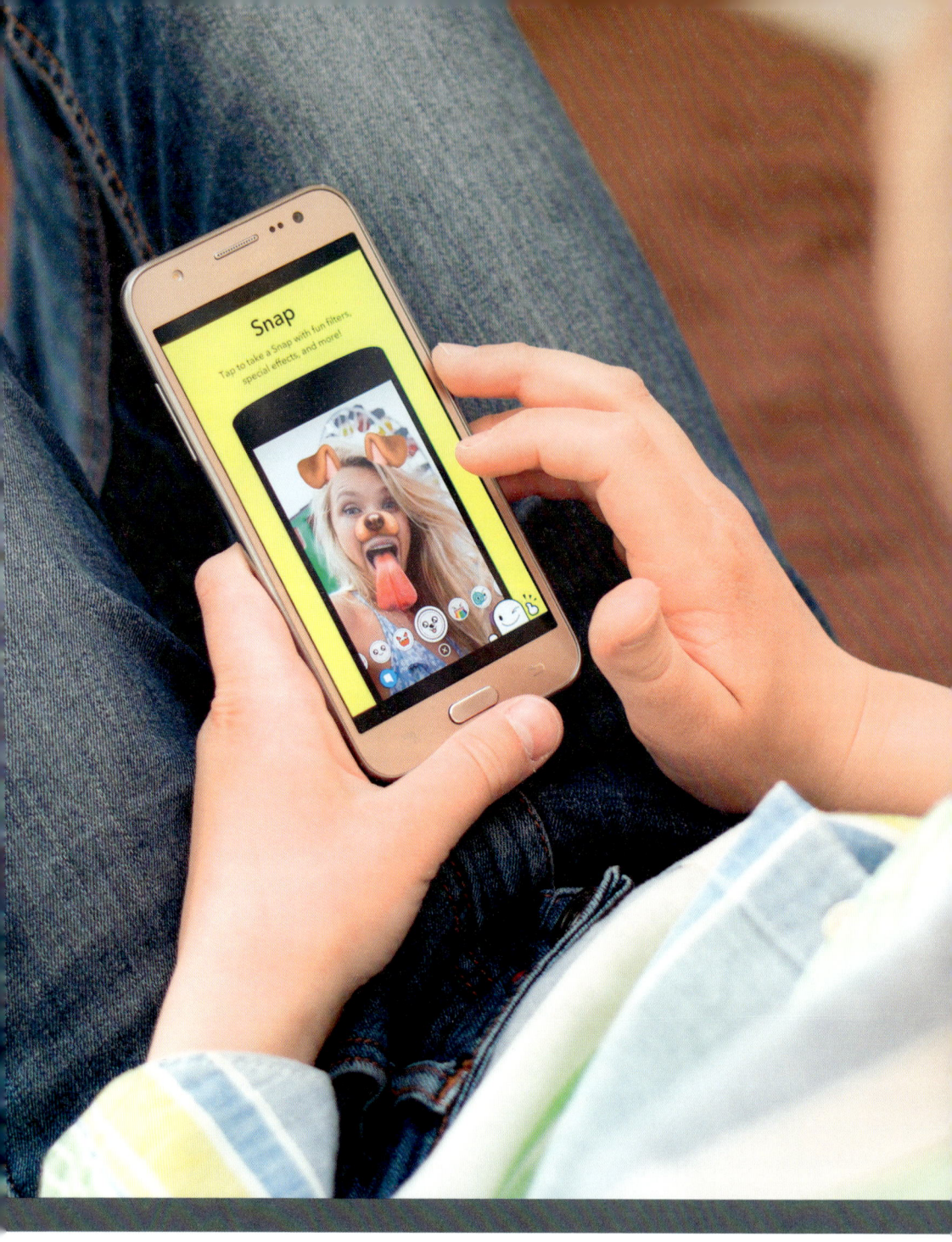
Snapchat can become addictive for some young users.

share **explicit** content or bully others on Snapchat. The app also made it easier for kids to hide their social media activity from their parents.

Another feature of Snapchat is Snapstreaks. Sending someone Snaps for two or more days starts a Snapstreak. Users are encouraged to keep a Snapstreak going. This makes the app **addictive** for some young people. But others may feel pressured. They worry about letting their friends down if they do not send Snaps often enough. This can become stressful for some users.

CHAPTER TWO

HOW DOES SOCIAL MEDIA AFFECT INDIVIDUALS?

Social media can have a big effect on a person's **self-image**. When users get positive responses, they often feel good about themselves. A person who posts a photo may get many likes from online friends. Some friends might even

Some social media users feel upset or embarrassed if a post gets a low number of likes.

post flattering comments. These responses often make a user feel more confident. But there is often a need for more and more positive attention.

Many social media users hope their posts will get lots of likes. If their posts do not get likes, some users start feeling bad about themselves. Some users even delete posts that do not get any likes. They feel too embarrassed to leave the posts up. It does

---

FILTERED IMAGES

Filters change the way photos look. Some apps have fun filters. For example, some filters add cat ears or puppy noses to selfies. But other filters try to make people look prettier. People use them because it feels good to post flattering pictures. But experts say filters can create unrealistic standards. Many young women feel pressured to look like these highly edited images. This can lead to depression or suicidal thoughts.

not even matter if their other posts have gotten lots of likes. Dr. Pamela Rutledge is a psychologist. She explained, "People who suffer from low self-esteem may continue to search for a feeling of worthiness online."[3] She added that these people focus too much on how many likes they get. They think getting a low number of likes means they are not good enough.

CONSTANT COMPARISONS

Some mental health experts think selfies are harmful to young people. These photos have become very popular on social media. Some users take lots of selfies. They worry

Selfies can cause teens to feel insecure about the way they look.

about posting the best photo. Sometimes, they start to think that their photos are not as good as other images they see online. This makes users feel bad. It can lead many teens to be too **critical** of the way they look.

Even users who get lots of likes can feel insecure about their looks. Users may post selfies to get likes. But the likes do not change how they see themselves. They still see things they do not like in the selfies. But they keep posting more photos. This can become a harmful cycle. It is especially common among teenage girls.

It can be even worse for young people who live with a mental illness. Psychologists say that people who are depressed or anxious are more likely to compare themselves to others or devalue themselves. One study looked at girls who

Selfies can make people feel pressured to look perfect. They can negatively impact teens, especially young girls or people who have a mental illness.

use Facebook. It found that girls who spend

more time looking at selfies become less

satisfied with their weight. Some girls work hard to look perfect. This can make them more likely to develop an eating disorder.

REAL LIFE VERSUS ONLINE IMAGES

Teens often compare their activities and accomplishments with those of their online friends. It may seem like other people are always doing something fun. One friend is celebrating a birthday. Another is taking an exciting vacation. Someone else may be winning a playoff game. Most people post only things that paint a positive picture of their lives. Many people feel like their real lives cannot keep up with the things

Many social media users share exciting vacation pictures on social media. People often end up comparing these photos to their own everyday lives.

that users share online. They often end up feeling sad or jealous.

Social media itself does not cause mental health problems. But it can trigger feelings that are hard for some people to manage. Dr. Olivia Remes studies mental health. She told *Vogue*, "When we're comparing our true reality to other people's rosy, Instagrammable lives, our own shortcomings begin to stand out. This can make you feel dissatisfied about your own life, inferior, and depressed."[4]

FEAR OF MISSING OUT

Some young people see social media as an important way to connect with friends. Many social gatherings that take place in real life are planned online. If someone spends less time online, they could get left out. People have a name for this fear. They call it FOMO. This stands for "fear of missing out."

SPENDING TOO MUCH TIME ON SOCIAL MEDIA

People who spend more time on social media are at greater risk for many mental health problems. Experts say users should spend less than 30 minutes per day on social media. Heavy social media use could lead to anxiety, depression, and self-harm.

Being social is usually a positive thing. But there is a difference between spending time with people in person and communicating with people on social media. Spending time with other people can make a person feel happier and less

Spending too much time on social media can lead to mental health problems.

lonely. But spending too much time on social media can make users feel lonelier. They can start feeling sad or frustrated. Users should think about taking a break when they feel this way.

People can even become addicted to social media. Getting likes or positive

Social media can be addictive and distracting. People addicted to social media might neglect their friends or favorite activities.

comments can cause an emotional reaction. It triggers the release of **dopamine** in the user's brain. This is the same chemical that is released when a gambler wins money. The release feels like a reward. The user wants to be rewarded again. So he will keep checking the social media account. Each like makes him want to keep checking. People who become addicted put social media first. They will spend time on social media even when it means neglecting other parts of their lives.

HARMING REAL-LIFE RELATIONSHIPS

Many people use social media to make their social circles bigger. But it can hurt real-life relationships. For instance, a person might use social media apps while spending time with family and friends. This makes those face-to-face interactions less meaningful. A user's loved ones may feel ignored. The user also misses out in this situation. She might feel distracted and less engaged with the people around her.

CHAPTER THREE

HOW DOES SOCIAL MEDIA AFFECT SOCIETY?

Social media has brought society together in many fun ways. Family and friends who live far apart find it useful and enjoyable. These people once relied on phone calls and visits to keep in touch. Now they can keep up with loved ones on

Social media allows people to stay connected with family and friends.

their phones and computers. Social media has made it feel like their loved ones are not so far away. It can make family and friends feel like they are still part of fun times. This sense of togetherness is one of the positive effects of social media.

Social media also helps many people make new friends. It makes it easy to meet people and build new friendships. It has become a way for people to connect with existing friends, as well.

TOO MANY FRIENDS

Research shows that most people can keep up with about 150 relationships. But many people have far more than 150 social media friends. Having lots of social media connections makes many people feel liked. But having lots of connections does not mean having lots of real friendships. People with more than 150 social media connections usually do not have meaningful connections with all those people.

Both large and small businesses use social media to advertise new products or research what customers like.

DOING BUSINESS ON SOCIAL MEDIA

Today, many businesses have at least one social media page. Posting to platforms such as Facebook and Instagram is an effective form of advertising. Customers can follow a business on social media.

Social media has changed how people experience online shopping. Many social media users enjoy interacting with brands and seeing ads for items they might like.

This makes it easy for the company to alert them to new products and sales. Businesses can also do research on social media. A post can ask users about which products or services they are interested in.

Social media has made online shopping easier too. People can click ads to make purchases. Customers can even use social media to get in touch with a business. In the past, customers had to call the company and wait to speak with someone. Now they can often send a direct message to ask a question.

Social media has turned online shopping into a more personal experience. Jamie Gilpin works for a company that helps businesses manage their social media accounts. She says that customers "expect brands to interact with them in meaningful

Many social media apps track users' interests and show them targeted ads. This can cause users to overspend.

ways and know them better based on their social media activity."5 Many social media users like seeing ads for items that match their interests.

But some people do not like the link between social media and retailers.

Many people want to keep their social media browsing separate from their shopping habits. They do not want their information shared with retailers. They feel this takes away their privacy.

Social media can also tempt many users to overspend. Ads on social media often target users' interests. Many apps track what users post about. Then they guide users toward products that match their interests. Many users also feel pressure to compete with friends on social media. A 2018 study looked at how social media affects the spending habits of **millennials**.

It found that social media led 57 percent of them to spend money on things they had not planned on buying.

THE CAMBRIDGE ANALYTICA SCANDAL

Cambridge Analytica was a company that helped businesses and political parties grow their audiences. In 2016, it got access to 87 million Facebook profiles. The company did this by creating an online quiz. When users took the quiz, Cambridge Analytica got information about them. This included where users lived and what Facebook pages they liked. The company worked with Donald Trump's presidential campaign. It targeted voters with ads based on this information. When people found out about this, many became concerned about their privacy on social media.

Social media has changed the way many people get news.

THE WAY PEOPLE GET NEWS

Before social media, people had to buy newspapers or turn on a television to get news. Now they can scroll social media to see what is happening in the world. Most news organizations have websites and apps that people can check whenever they like. But this takes some effort. On social media, users can follow news accounts. Headlines become a part of the user's feed. When something happens, they see posts about it almost instantly.

The type of news that a user gets depends on the accounts she follows. The news that appears on a person's feed also depends on how popular a story is. The more likes a story gets, the more it will appear in other people's social media feeds. Users can also share news stories with friends.

When people get news on social media, they are not always getting the whole story. The average user spends fifteen seconds or less reading a news article on social media. Users may spend just ten seconds watching a news video. When they want to

GETTING NEWS FROM NON-NEWS SOURCES

By 2019, about half of teens were getting news from social media apps at least a few times a week. Often, the information was not reliable. Nearly all news networks post articles to Facebook and Instagram. But six out of ten teens said they were more likely to get their news from celebrities or influencers than news organizations.

Fake news is a major problem on social media. It can be hard to tell if information is true or false.

know more about a story, users often go to the news organization's website. Social media has increased the number of people who visit news websites.

One of the biggest problems with news on social media is fake news. This is content that is created to mislead users. Many social media accounts look like real news organizations. But they are really individuals or companies who are trying to influence people. They do this by posting misleading content. Many fake news stories are about politics. But a fake story can be about anything. When users share stories on social media, it can sometimes add to this problem. A 2019 study looked at social media users who share news online. Nearly half of them had passed on a fake story.

CYBERBULLYING

Social media comments are not always friendly. Arguments can get out of control quickly. They can even include cyberbullying. Lydia Denworth is an author and journalist. She says, "Mean girls and bullies were not invented with the iPhone, although their potential reach has expanded exponentially."[6] When conflicts happen on social media, they are usually seen by a lot more people than when they happen in person.

Cyberbullying is one of the most harmful problems that social media has

Many kids and teens have experienced cyberbullying on social media.

brought to society. It can include personal attacks, spreading private information, or even discrimination. Research shows that 90 percent of teens in the United States think that cyberbullying is a problem for their

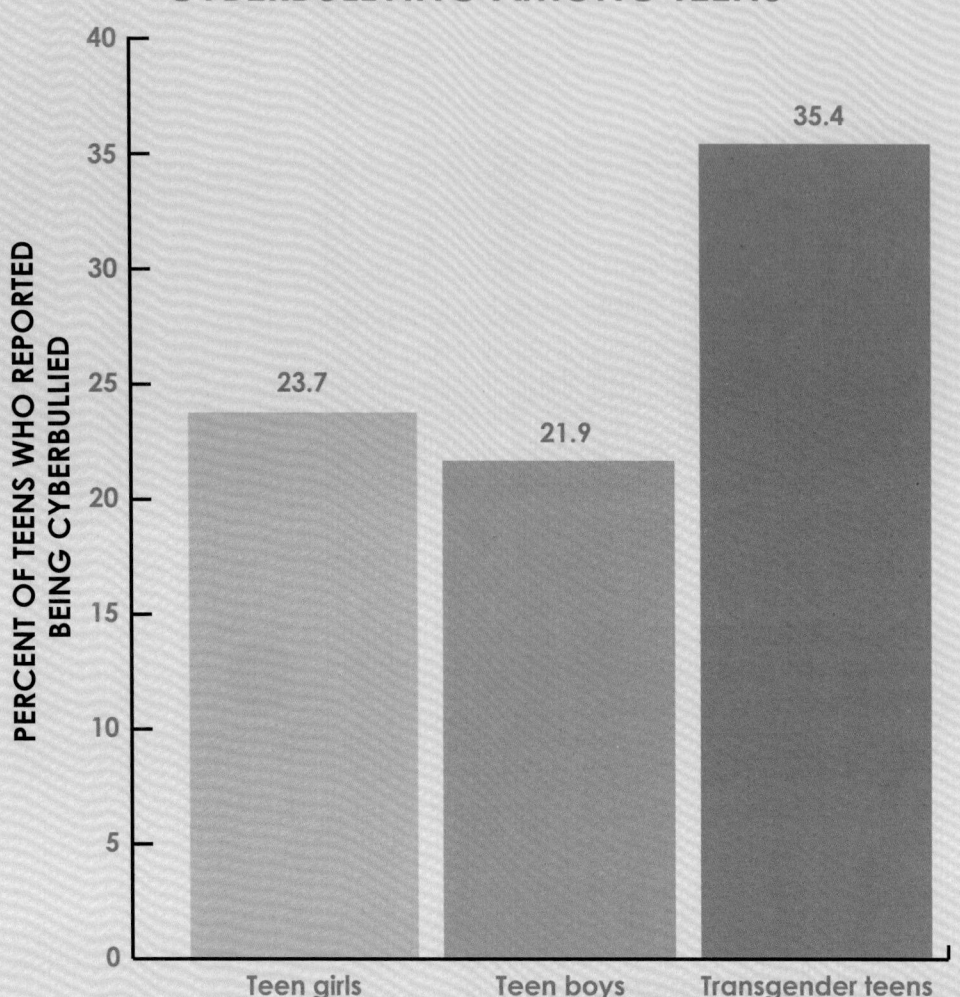

In a 2021 survey, both teen girls and boys reported being cyberbullied. But more girls and transgender teens said they had faced this problem.

age group. And 59 percent say they have been victims of it. Most young people also think that social media companies are not doing enough to stop the problem.

Certain groups are more likely than others to be targets of cyberbullying. Members of the **LGBTQ** community and people from lower-income households have a higher risk of getting bullied. Shy or socially awkward kids are also more likely to be targeted. But anyone can be cyberbullied. Even celebrities and other public figures are bullied by some social media users.

CHAPTER FOUR

HOW IS SOCIAL MEDIA CHANGING FOR THE BETTER?

Some social media companies are trying to make their platforms more positive spaces. For example, Facebook has added tools that allow users to report bullying on the platform. Before, users could report people who bullied them. But now,

Some social media platforms have created new tools to fight cyberbullying. They encourage users to report bullying when they see it happen online.

users can speak up if they see other people getting bullied. In many cases, victims of bullying do not feel comfortable reporting the problem. They may worry about bullies getting angry. Facebook hopes that letting anyone report the problem will encourage all users to help stop cyberbullying.

In 2021, Instagram started letting users turn off the like counts on their posts. This means that a user's followers cannot see how many people like her photos. The goal is to lessen the pressure users feel to get likes. Adam Mosseri is the head of Instagram. He said, "The more we can give people the ability to shape Instagram and Facebook into what's good for them, the better."[7]

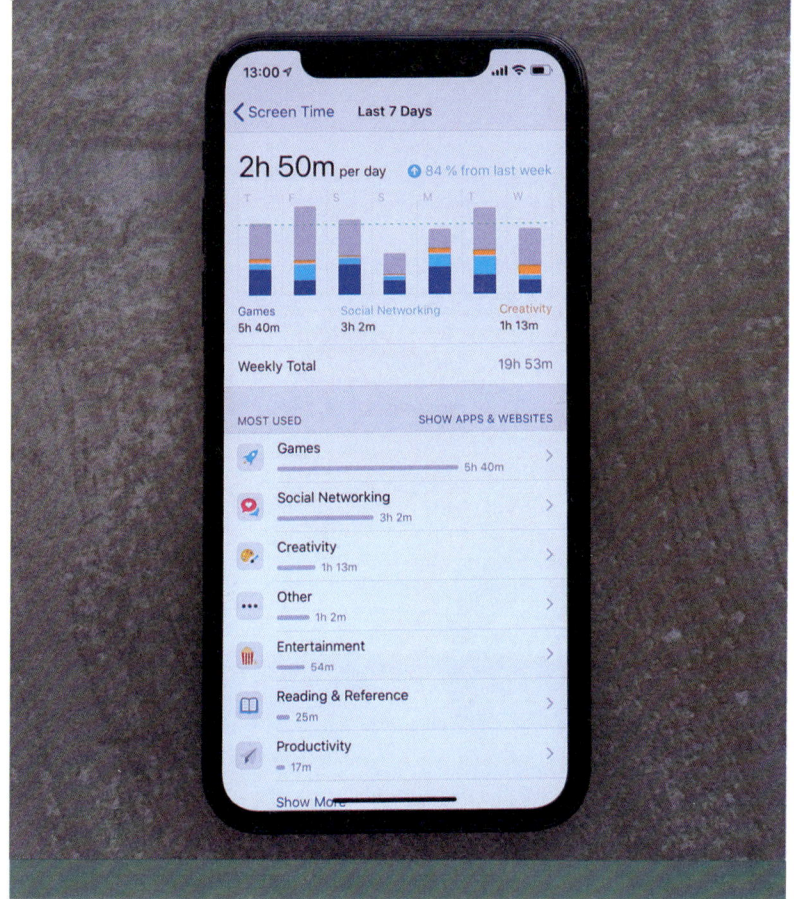

People can use control settings on their phones to limit the amount of time they spend on social media.

CHANGES SOCIAL MEDIA USERS CAN MAKE

There are lots of tools that can make social media safer and more positive for users. But the people who have the most control

A social media detox can help users overcome social media addiction.

are users themselves. One of the best ways to make social media a healthier experience is limiting the amount of time spent on it. This can keep social media from affecting the way users spend the rest of their time.

Many smartphones even have control settings that can help. When a user reaches a time limit on an app, the app will alert the user. Other people find it helpful to turn off their notifications. They may choose to check their social media accounts only at certain times of day.

Users who spend too much time on social media can also try a social media **detox**. This is a break from all social media. A detox can feel extreme at first. But it can help users overcome an addiction. Jane Pernotto Ehrman is a behavioral health therapist. She explained that users who detox do not have to leave social media forever. She said, "Stepping away from social media is a great way to get a better picture of reality. . . . The whole idea is that you're just more aware of it."[8]

IGNORE, DELETE, OR BLOCK AS NEEDED

Negative people can be hard to deal with on social media. The best thing to do is ignore them. But that can be hard to do when their posts regularly appear on one's feed. Most social media apps have features that can help with this problem. The first option is to unfollow people who post stressful content. On some apps,

Unfollowing people who post negative content can make a user's social media experience healthier.

users can stop seeing a person's content without unfriending them. Unfollowing can be helpful when the other person is a family member or close friend in real life.

Unfollowing certain news outlets, online magazines, or celebrities can be useful too.

But sometimes unfollowing is not enough. For example, most social media platforms allow users to send direct messages. If these messages cause stress

BEING UNFRIENDED

It can be difficult to get unfriended by someone on social media. The healthiest way to deal with the situation is by not thinking about it too much. If the person was a close friend, it might help to ask her what caused the problem. Being respectful to others both online and in the real world is the best way to prevent the situation. But sometimes users get unfriended even when they did nothing wrong.

or other harmful emotions, it may be best to unfriend the user. In some cases, blocking the user may also be a good idea. If a person is getting bullied, blocking the bully is a smart step to stop communication.

Users can also change their social media settings to limit contact with specific people. Facebook lets users share their posts with certain friends. Instagram allows users to limit comments to a certain number. They can also turn comments off completely. These steps can make social media less stressful.

SPREADING POSITIVITY

Social media can be used for good too. Following accounts that share positive messages can be inspiring. Users can share stories, cute animal photos, or funny memes. A smile or a good laugh can help fight the negativity found on social media.

Social media users can be part of the change they hope to see on social media. A quick hello between friends who have not talked in a while can brighten both people's days. Posting an inspiring quote can also spread positivity. Some social media platforms even make it easy for

Sharing uplifting stories, funny pictures, or kind messages is a great way to spread positivity on social media.

users to raise money for charity. A user can pick a charity for friends to donate to on his birthday.

Social media has its downsides. But it can also add positive social interactions

When people use social media in a healthy way, it can add positive interactions to their lives.

to people's lives. Experts agree that there are ways to make social media a healthier experience. Users can limit their time on the apps. They can spread positive messages. These steps are the best way to keep social media as healthy as possible.

A SOCIAL MEDIA APP WITH LIMITS

An app called BeReal was released in 2020. BeReal gives users only two minutes each day for posting. People can share one post per day. The exact time they can post changes each day too. Users cannot use filters or edit their photos. There is no like button. Friends can only see content if they share a photo themselves. Many people think the app encourages users to be more genuine. That is why it is called BeReal.

GLOSSARY

addictive

causing a person to use or do something too long or too often

critical

finding fault or flaws in something

detox

an intentional break from an unhealthy habit

dopamine

a brain chemical that causes a feeling of pleasure

explicit

of a graphic or sexual nature

LGBTQ

lesbian, gay, bisexual, transgender, and queer

millennials

a group of people who reached adulthood in the early 2000s

online predators

people who try to connect with others online so they can abuse or harm them

self-image

the ideas a person has about one's own strengths and weaknesses

SOURCE NOTES

CHAPTER ONE: HOW DID SOCIAL MEDIA START?

1. Quoted in Jon Miller and Aisha Sultan, "'Facebook Parenting' Is Destroying Our Children's Privacy," *CNN*, May 25, 2012. www.cnn.com.

2. Quoted in Robert T. Muller, "Social Media Affects Influencers' Mental Health," *Psychology Today*, October 6, 2021. www.psychologytoday.com.

CHAPTER TWO: HOW DOES SOCIAL MEDIA AFFECT INDIVIDUALS?

3. Quoted in Sarah Z. Wexler, "Why Your Likes Don't Actually Mean Anything," *Cosmopolitan*, June 3, 2016. www.cosmopolitan.com.

4. Quoted in Tish Weinstock, "Why Can't I Stop Comparing Myself to Other People on Instagram?" *Vogue*, March 20, 2021. www.vogue.in.

CHAPTER THREE: HOW DOES SOCIAL MEDIA AFFECT SOCIETY?

5. Quoted in Gary Drenik, "Businesses Are Increasing Their Investments in Social Media as Consumers Use Social Media More Than Ever Before – Here's Why," *Forbes*, April 22, 2021. www.forbes.com.

6. Quoted in Lydia Denworth, "Why the Digital Age Is Not Destroying Friendship," *Forge*, January 24, 2020. https://forge.medium.com.

CHAPTER FOUR: HOW IS SOCIAL MEDIA CHANGING FOR THE BETTER?

7. Quoted in Cristina Criddle, "Instagram Lets Users Hide Likes to Reduce Social Media Pressure," *BBC News*, May 26, 2021. www.bbc.com.

8. Quoted in "8 Signs You Need to Take a Break from Social Media," *Cleveland Clinic: Health Essentials*, November 5, 2020. https://health.clevelandclinic.org.

FOR FURTHER RESEARCH

BOOKS

Ruth Bennett and Sarah Eason, *How Do I Manage My Social Media?* Minneapolis, MN: Lerner, 2022.

Tammy Gagne, *How Social Media Impacts News*. San Diego, CA: BrightPoint Press, 2021.

Heather C. Hudak, *Cell Phone Privacy*. Minneapolis, MN: Abdo Publishing, 2019.

INTERNET SOURCES

"Is Social Media Good for Society?" *Time for Kids*, January 23, 2020. www.timeforkids.com.

"Social Media," *National Cybersecurity Alliance*, n.d. https://staysafeonline.org.

"Staying Safe on Social Media," *Kidscape*, n.d. www.kidscape.org.uk.

WEBSITES

FBI: Safe Online Surfing
https://sos.fbi.gov

FBI: Safe Online Surfing helps students learn about being safe online. It offers games for different grade levels and an internet safety test.

Safe Search Kids
www.safesearchkids.com

Safe Search Kids is a custom search engine that helps kids do online searches with less risk. It blocks harmful content from users.

StopBullying.gov
www.stopbullying.gov

StopBullying.gov helps kids understand what cyberbullying is and who is at risk of getting cyberbullied. It also covers ways to prevent cyberbullying and how to report it.

INDEX

addiction, 27, 39–41, 65–66
advertising, 22–23, 45–46, 47–50

BeReal, 73
Bloch, Jamie, 23–25
blocking, 68–69
businesses, 22, 45–49

Cambridge Analytica, 50
cyberbullying, 15, 56–59, 60–62, 69

Denworth, Lydia, 56
dopamine, 40–41

Facebook, 16–20, 34, 45, 50, 53, 60–62, 69
fake accounts, 15–16
fake news, 55
filters, 30, 73

Gilpin, Jamie, 47–48

influencers, 22–25, 53
Instagram, 21–23, 45, 53, 62, 69

LGBTQ community, 58, 59
likes, 28–31, 33, 39–41, 52, 62, 73

mental health, 10, 30, 31–37, 38–39
Mosseri, Adam, 62
Myspace, 13–16

news accounts, 51–55, 68

online predators, 15–16
online shopping, 47–50
overspending, 49–50

Pernotto Ehrman, Jane, 65–66
privacy, 15–18, 49, 50, 57

Remes, Olivia, 37
Rutledge, Pamela, 31

selfies, 22, 30, 31–35
self-image, 28–35, 36–37
Snapchat, 25–27
Snapstreaks, 27
social media detoxes, 65–66

TikTok, 24

unfollowing, 66–68
unfriending, 68–69

IMAGE CREDITS

Cover: © Backgroundy/Shutterstock Images
5: © Casarsa Guru/iStockphoto
7: © Marcos Calvo/iStockphoto
8: © Raw Pixel/Shutterstock Images
10: © Kali 9/iStockphoto
13: © Art Of Photos/Shutterstock Images
14: © Big Tuna Online/Shutterstock Images
17: © Prostock Studio/Shutterstock Images
18: © Sol Stock/iStockphoto
21: © Grinvalds/iStockphoto
23: © Olesiabilkei/iStockphoto
26: © Alesia Kan/Shutterstock Images
29: © Katarzyna Bialasiewicz/iStockphoto
32: © China Face/iStockphoto
34: © Alex Maryna/Shutterstock Images
36: © Sasin Paraksa/Shutterstock Images
39: © Tatyana GI/iStockphoto
40: © BAZA Production/Shutterstock Images
43: © Aleksandra Suzi/Shutterstock Images
45: © Asia Vision/iStockphoto
46: © Goroden Koff/iStockphoto
48: © Chaay Tee/iStockphoto
51: © Casimiro PT/Shutterstock Images
54: © Anchiy/iStockphoto
57: © Fizkes/Shutterstock Images
61: © Three Spots/iStockphoto
63: © Cristian Dina/Shutterstock Images
64: © New Africa/Shutterstock Images
67: © Trzykropy/Shutterstock Images
71: © Light Field Studios/Shutterstock Images
72: © Artist GND photography/iStockphoto

ABOUT THE AUTHOR

Tammy Gagne has written hundreds of books for both adults and children. Some of her recent books have been about gaming disorder and media bias. She lives in northern New England with her husband, son, and dogs.